The of the Missing Glass Slipper

by Daphne Greaves
illustrated by Michela Galassi

Harcourt
SCHOOL PUBLISHERS

Printed in China

ISBN 10: 0-15-350487-0
ISBN 13: 978-0-15-350487-7

Ordering Options
ISBN 10: 0-15-350333-5 (Grade 3 Below-Level Collection)
ISBN 13: 978-0-15-350333-7 (Grade 3 Below-Level Collection)
ISBN 10: 0-15-357473-9 (package of 5)
ISBN 13: 978-0-15-357473-3 (package of 5)

2 3 4 5 6 7 8 9 10 985 12 11 10 09 08 07

Characters:

Narrator	**Cinderella**
Prince	**Stepmother**
Officer Hunter	**Fairy Godmother**

Setting: A fairy tale kingdom

Narrator: Once upon a time there lived a very charming prince.

Prince: Officer Hunter, thank you for coming.

Officer Hunter: That's my job, Prince Charming.

Officer Hunter: Prince, what seems to be the trouble?

Narrator: Last night, the prince held a huge banquet. The scent of the food was delicious! Everyone was invited. The prince wandered from table to table. He danced like an expert with various ladies. Then, it happened.

Prince: I was dancing with a young lady. Suddenly, she turned and ran out the door! I need to find her. When she ran away, she lost this glass slipper.

Officer Hunter: Why don't you put an ad in the paper?

Prince: That would alert the media, and I don't want her to be embarrassed. It would also be more charming to take the slipper to her.

Officer Hunter: I will investigate and try to find some clues.

Prince: Will you need the police laboratory to run tests?

Officer Hunter: Probably not.

Narrator: Officer Hunter took photos of some tiny footprints outside the palace.

Officer Hunter: Look at the right toe print. It's deeper than the left. That could be a clue.

Narrator: He looked at the glass slipper.

Officer Hunter: It's the smallest slipper I've ever seen.

Prince: There's the name of a shoe store on the slipper.

Officer Hunter: Fairy Godmother Shoe Store. Come on!

Officer Hunter: Are you Fairy Godmother?

Fairy Godmother: Yes, I am.

Officer Hunter: Do you know who bought this shoe?

Fairy Godmother: I suspect I know. Only one person I know has such a tiny foot, but I'm afraid I can't give out that information.

Officer Hunter: We're not just asking out of curiosity.

Prince: I want to return the slipper to the owner.

Fairy Godmother: I'm sorry. That information is secret. I could return it for you.

Prince: I want to return it myself. It's the charming thing to do.

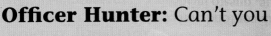

Officer Hunter: Can't you give us a clue?

Fairy Godmother: I really shouldn't, but the prince is so charming that I will. The owner of the slipper lives in town.

Narrator: The two began searching. They knocked on a cottage door. Cinderella lived there with her mean stepmother.

Stepmother: Cinderella, answer the door!

Narrator: A very nice girl in shabby clothes opened the door.

Cinderella: May I help you?

Officer Hunter: I'm Officer Hunter, and this is Prince Charming.

Stepmother: Prince Charming! Do come in!

Prince: That's very generous of you.

Stepmother: What a charming man! How can I help you?

Prince: We're looking for the owner of this slipper.

Officer Hunter: Perhaps it belongs to the young lady.

Stepmother: Cinderella? She'd never wear anything so lovely.

Officer Hunter: You do have a small foot, young lady. Are you sure it's not your slipper?

Cinderella: I'm sorry, but I must get back to my sweeping.

11

Stepmother: I told you it's not hers. Now go flick those ashes into the bin, Cinderella.

Narrator: Officer Hunter watched as Cinderella swept up ashes. He noticed the footprints she made on the dirty floor. Hunter knew he had to get the stepmother out of the room.

Officer Hunter: We need to see your best shoes.

Stepmother: Now?

Hunter: Right now.

Narrator: Stepmother ran upstairs to get her best shoes. Then Officer Hunter showed Cinderella the photo of footprints he took earlier. They perfectly matched the footprints in the ashes.

Cinderella: I confess! The slipper is mine.

Prince: Why did you run away last night?

Cinderella: Stepmother gets home by midnight. I had to get home before she did.

Prince: So it wasn't anything I did?

13

Cinderella: Oh, no! You were very charming.

Prince: No, I wasn't.

Cinderella: Yes, you were.

Prince: No, I wasn't—

Narrator: Anyway! The prince returned the slipper. Meanwhile, Officer Hunter was very impressed with Cinderella. In fact, he offered her a job. Cinderella accepted, and they all lived happily ever after.

Think Critically

1. What does Prince Charming want Officer Hunter to do?

2. On page 4, the Narrator says that the prince *wandered* from table to table. What does the word *wandered* mean?

3. What does Stepmother think of Cinderella?

4. How does Officer Hunter get Stepmother out of the room?

5. Do you think Prince Charming is charming or silly? Explain your answer.

 Language Arts

Make a List Officer Hunter followed different clues to find Cinderella. Take a piece of paper. Write "Clues" at the top of the page. Write a sentence about each clue that Officer Hunter used to find Cinderella.

School-Home Connection Borrow the fairy tale "Cinderella" from the library. Read it aloud with a friend or family member.

Word Count: 671